Hello I'm Kath.

I work in schools, preschools and nurseries running Relax Kids courses and I also offer family sessions/1-2-1s. I also run an online Relaxation on a Monday for adults - https://bit.ly/mon-med.

I also have a relaxation gift box for adults and an anxiety gift box for adults - https://bit.ly/meditationbox.

I live with my husband Rob, our 2 girls Jasmine and Phoebe and Jasmine's Hamster "Hollie" (who is the star of this book). We live in Basingstoke in Hampshire.

Introduction for Parents

The idea behind this book is to support children in the run up to starting school as well as through the early days of starting school and beyond.

It can feel quite daunting starting school for many children. And it can feel equally daunting for the parents too (actually these exercises can be applied to all age groups in times of anxiety). The idea with this book is that you and your child become familiar with these techniques so that they become second nature by the time your child starts school and of course they can be continued on their journey through education.

I wanted this book to provide several scenarios with techniques alongside. It is not possible for the book to cover all scenarios that children might be faced with but I hope you find it helpful.

The illustrations are deliberately low key so that the focus is on the strategies.

Disclaimer

This book is intended to offer strategies for children to use in those moments that they find tricky.

With the breathing exercises please encourage children to listen to their body and do what feels right for them. If a breathing exercise doesn't feel comfortable then perhaps try again another time.

It may be that the methods might not help the first time your child uses them but with regular practice I'm hopeful that they will help.

Sometimes we might still feel worried even after practicing the techniques in this book but that doesn't mean they aren't working. We might just need to keep that exercise in our mind and practice again later.

And now we start with an introduction to Hollie Hamster

Hollie is Jasmine's hamster. Hollie came to live with us in May 2021 and she has been lots of fun.

Hollie loves running in her wheel, eating carrots and climbing. She especially loves climbing and often tries to escape from her cage.

Here is Hollie.

Hollie Hamster woke up with a funny feeling in her tummy. A bit like butterflies flying around inside. She was feeling a little bit nervous as she lay in bed. She also felt something else but she wasn't quite sure what. Then she remembered that it was her first day at school. Hollie realised that she felt a teeny tiny bit excited too as she jumped out of bed.

Hollie Hamster remembered that there was something she could do when she felt the funny feeling like butterflies in her tummy. She knew a great way to really help herself feel a little bit better.

I wonder what Hollie Hamster is going to do.....

Using her imagination Hollie Hamster started to pretend she was first smelling a flower and then blowing bubbles. This helped her to think about breathing in through her nose and out through her mouth.

Hollie Hamster knew that practicing this exercise would help her when she felt a little bit nervous and a little bit excited at the same time.

Can you try this breathing exercise if you start to feel a little bit nervous and a little bit excited at the same time? Why don't you practice this breathing exercise now?

"Good morning Hollie" her Mummy said, coming into her room. "It's time to wake up and get ready for school".

"I'm up already" Hollie said. "I'm a little bit excited but I'm a little bit scared too".

"It's perfectly fine and quite normal to feel a little bit excited and a little bit anxious or scared at the same time when we are about to do something new. I expect there are lots of hamsters that feel the same way as you. Do you remember another time that you felt nervous and excited at the same time".

I wonder if Hollie Hamster can remember.....

"Yes Mummy, when we went to the big rides at the funfair, it all looked quite scary and I remember feeling a bit scared and a bit excited at the same time. But I tried the big rides and they were fun."

"Do you remember what you did before you went on the biggest ride Hollie?" asked Mummy "If you can why don't you try it now?"

"Yes, I remember Mummy" said Hollie. "I'm going to...."

I wonder what Hollie Hamster is going to do.....

I'm going to use
my positive words.

I am brave
I am brave
I am brave

Can you think of some
positive words that you
could use on your first
day at school?

Hollie then had her
breakfast and got
ready to go to school.

"Come on Hollie" said her Daddy when she was ready "it's time to go".

Hollie's Mummy kissed her on the cheek and told her that she would be thinking of her all day and that she wanted to hear all about what she did at school when she came home.

"I'm really going to miss you and Daddy" said Hollie

"Have you remembered what we did last week Hollie? We knew how much we'd miss each other."

I wonder what Hollie Hamster and her Mummy did last week.....

"Do you remember, Hollie, we each coloured a heart shape and we put them in the cupboard ready for today. Shall I get them?"

Hollie's Mummy went to the cupboard to get the hearts that they had coloured last week.

Hollie took the heart that Mummy had coloured and put it in her bag. Mummy popped the heart that Hollie had coloured in her pocket.

Can you draw a heart that you can give to your grown up and ask them to draw a heart for you to put in your bag?

On her way to school Hollie Hamster remembered what Mummy had said about school. She had said that school was a fun place where Hollie would meet lots of new friends.

Hollie still felt a little nervous about leaving her home. At school she would not have her Mummy or Daddy around. Would she really be ok?

Hollie Hamster knew that they had been practicing helpful things to make her feel safe and calm. But goodness me, she couldn't remember them!

Then she saw something that reminded her of what she could do. In a window she saw a rainbow.

I wonder what Hollie Hamster is going to do.....

Hollie Hamster remembered that noticing the colours of the rainbow would help take her mind off of how she was feeling.

So now she had to try and remember the colours of the rainbow in order.

Do you know the colours of the rainbow?

Can you see the different colours around you?

See if you can spot something red? Can you spot something orange? How about something yellow? Now see if you can see green? And blue? And finally purple?

When they arrived at school, Hollie's Daddy talked a little with her teacher, Miss Siri. Then he gave Hollie a kiss on the cheek and a thumbs-up. Then he left.

Miss Siri, Hollie's teacher, said that Hollie's bale of hay was in the second row near the window. Miss Siri also said that in a moment she would tell everyone what they would be doing that week and if they forgot anything they could put their hand up.

Hollie Hamster looked over and felt a little nervous again about going over and sitting next to someone she didn't know.

But she remembered something that she could do to help herself.

I wonder what Hollie Hamster is going to do.....

Hollie Hamster remembered another breathing exercise that she could practice. Rectangle breathing was going to be another good one to try. But uh-oh she couldn't quite remember what a rectangle looked like.

Do you know what a rectangle is?

If you don't why not ask your adult to draw one for you so that you can trace around it. Or use the one here.

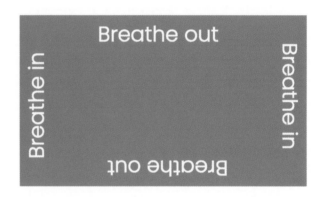

With rectangle breathing we pretend to draw a rectangle on our hands. Rectangles have 2 short sides and 2 long sides. As we draw the rectangle on our hand we breathe in for the short sides and breathe out for the long sides. Why don't you give it a go?

"Good morning hamsters" the teacher said when everyone was seated. "Welcome to school. I'm your class teacher, Miss Siri. I'm sure we are going to have a lot of fun today."

Hollie was pleased to hear that.

The teacher said that the hamsters would have to practice listening really well so that they didn't miss anything.

Hollie Hamster remembered a little exercise that she had tried before and it was a great one to help her concentrate.

I wonder what Hollie Hamster is going to do.....

Hollie Hamster remembered a listening exercise that she had practiced and got really good at. She remembered she had to sit super, super still and notice any sounds going on around her.

She always tried to notice 3 different sounds.

Do you think you can sit super quietly and super still and notice any sounds going on around you?

What did you hear?
How many different
sounds did you hear?

Soon it was time for a break and Hollie Hamster was really starting to miss her Mummy and Daddy.

Then she remembered that she had the heart that her Mummy had coloured and because it was break time she could go and peek in her bag and look at it.

It helped her a little bit but she still felt a little bit sad about missing Mummy and Daddy.

Hollie knew that it was ok to feel sad but she also knew that she could do something to help herself when she felt sad. So she thought about something else she could do.

I wonder what Hollie Hamster is going to do.....

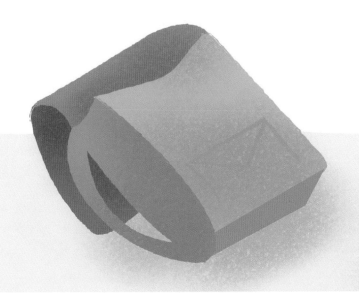

Hollie Hamster remembered a breathing exercise that she could do to help her when she felt a little sad. She was going to practice her breathing and count at the same time.

Hollie Hamster started using the numbers 1, 2 and 3 and all she did was breathe in and count to 1 and breathe out and count to 1. Then breathe in and count to 2 and breathe out and count to 2 and then breathe in and count to 3 and breathe out and count to 3.

Do you think you could try that one too?

At lunchtime Hollie was a bit worried about who she might play with. She didn't really know anyone apart from the friend she made this morning – Jasmine Hamster. She was sat with Jasmine all morning and she was very friendly but she couldn't see her right now.

Hollie remembered what Daddy had said about meeting new people and what she could do to make new friends.

Hollie decided she would go up to the hamsters stood together near the play area and .....

I wonder what Hollie Hamster is going to do.....

....ask them a question. That's exactly what Daddy had said to try. Between them they had come up with 2 questions that she could ask her new school friends.

Can you think of 2 questions that you might ask your new school friends before we find out what Hollie's questions are?

The first question Hollie Hamster asked her new friends was "what is your name?"

The second question Hollie Hamster asked her new friends was "do you like playing tag?"

Once Hollie Hamster's school friends answered, Hollie Hamster realised that it was a lot easier than she had thought before she started school. She was pleased to make a new friend called Phoebe Hamster.

She would definitely try those questions again with new school friends especially if it meant she could play tag at lunchtime.

When Hollie Hamster got back into the classroom, after she had worn herself out playing tag, she needed to go to the toilet.

But Hollie Hamster had forgotten where the toilet was.

Hollie Hamster hoped she wasn't going to get told off for not remembering where things were.

Hollie remembered what her Mummy had said if she needed help.

I wonder what Hollie Hamster is going to do.....

Hollie Hamster put her hand up
and asked her teacher, Miss Siri, if
she could go to the toilet.

Miss Siri said "yes of
course you can Hollie".

Hollie Hamster felt a bit nervous
as she said "but I can't remember
where the toilet is."

"Don't worry" said Miss Siri, "I'll show
you. I don't expect you to
remember everything on your first
day in school.   We are here to help
you get used to being in school.

And remember that all the grown-
ups in class will remind everyone
where things are and what you
need to do because there is a lot
to find out about school, but we are
here to help."

Soon it was time to go home. Hollie Hamster went to get her coat and her bag and then she started to feel a bit scared. She couldn't remember how to get home.

Then the teacher called her name and said "come on Hollie, your Mummy is waiting for you".

"Of course" thought Hollie Hamster "I'm far too young to go home by myself. Mummy or Daddy will pick me up after school every day."

As Hollie Hamster ran over to her Mummy for a big hug, Mummy asked "so, tell me Hollie, how was your day?"

Hollie Hamster was so excited to say that she had a really good day and that she had practiced all the things that she had been learning with Mummy and Daddy.

She said that she was now able to help herself in those tricky moments and knew how to help herself feel calm when she really didn't feel calm at all.

"And do you know what was best of all Mummy?" said Hollie Hamster..... " it all worked. I made some new friends and I played tag."

Hollie Hamster had had such a busy first day at school that by the time she got home she was super tired.

She ate her dinner, had her bath, cleaned her teeth and then listened to her bedtime story and went straight to sleep.

She couldn't wait to go back to school the next day.

Thank you for reading 'Hollie Hamster Goes To School'. Keep an eye out as Hollie Hamster may go on some adventures, and if she does you'll find out about them on my website (www.kazaar.co.uk).

If you enjoyed this book you might like to check out the Yasmine Yogi and Phoebe Bee books which also have some strategies for supporting children. You can find these on my website too (www.kazaar.co.uk).

I also have lots of tips for children and adults on Pinterest so you can follow me there too. Just search for @kathr6789 and follow me so you don't miss anything!

This book was illustrated by Rich Coombes of Creatively Rich. You can find him at www.creativelyrich.co.uk.

Printed in Great Britain
by Amazon

26999327R00018